KU-222-295

# Pirate Patch

## and the

# Black Bonnet Attack

In which the heroic Pirate Patch and his capable crew outwit the villainous Bones and Jones

For Reuben
R.I.

...nna (Peg!)
N.R.

WORCESTERSHIRE
COUNTY COUNCIL

| | |
|---|---|
| 375 | |
| Bertrams | 19/08/2008 |
| | £8.99 |
| ST | |

Reading Consultant: Prue Goodwin, Lecturer in Literacy and
Children's Books at the University of Reading

ORCHARD BOOKS
338 Euston Road, London NW1 3BH
*Orchard Books Australia*
Hachette Children's Books
Level 17/207 Kent Street, Sydney NSW 2000

First published by Orchard Books in 2008
First paperback publication 2009

Text © Rose Impey 2008
Illustrations © Nathan Reed 2008

The rights of Rose Impey to be identified as the author and
Nathan Reed to be identified as the illustrator of this Work
have been asserted by them in accordance with the
Copyright, Designs and Patents Act, 1988.

A CIP catalogue record for this book is available from the British Library

ISBN 978 1 84362 974 0 (hardback)
ISBN 978 1 84362 982 5 (paperback)

1 3 5 7 9 10 8 6 4 2
Printed in China

Orchard Books is a division of Hachette Children's Books,
an Hachette Livre UK company.
www.hachettelivre.co.uk

# Pirate Patch

## and the

## Black Bonnet Attack

ROSE IMPEY ◆ NATHAN REED

ORCHARD BOOKS

Patch waved goodbye as his mum
and dad's ship sailed away.
"Be good!" they called.

THE HIS AND HERSPANIOLA

Patch didn't want to be *good*,
he wanted to be a pirate!
As soon as Mum and Dad were
out of sight . . .

. . . Patch set sail in his own little boat, with his own very *capable* crew.

Patch was the captain of *The
Little Pearl* and Granny Peg
was first mate. Peg could read
a map in a minute . . . if she
had her glasses on.

Pierre, the lookout, could raise a flag in a flash.

And Portside was the cleverest sea dog ever to sail the seven seas.

Patch and his crew sailed all day, looking for adventure. But all day, there was nothing to see . . . but sea!

Patch was *bored.*

Suddenly, Pierre spotted
a ship in the distance.

"Kippers and Codswallop!"
snarled Peg. "If it isn't *The Black Bonnet*."
The ship belonged to her old enemies: Billy Bones and Davy Jones.

Grrrrr.

"Whistling whelks," whistled Patch.
"An adventure at last."

In two shakes of Portside's tail, *The Little Pearl* sailed alongside *The Black Bonnet* and roped it in.

The ship looked deserted
and before Peg could say,
"Beware! It might
be a . . ."

. . . Patch had raced across the rope and fallen into one!

"Well, quiver my timbers! What have we here?" growled Bones. "A young whippersnapper to walk the plank," chuckled Jones.

Patch tried to be brave.
"You don't scare me,
you lily-livered layabouts,"
he told Bones and Jones.

Patch's loyal crew could only stand and watch as the pirates prepared to push Patch off the plank.

Just in time,
Portside came
up with
a clever plan.

The plan was to swap Peg's
precious treasure map for
their captain.

"Stop!" Peg called, waving
the map.

Bones and Jones smiled. They both had the same idea.

First they would get their hands on the map, *then* they would push Patch off the plank.

But, the minute they had the map in their hands, Bones and Jones began to fight – as usual.

While the two pirates
were busy, Patch took
his chance to escape.

*The Little Pearl* quickly set
sail, leaving the *villainous*
pair far behind.

But in no time Patch looked back and saw *The Black Bonnet* racing after them.

What did those scoundrels want now, he wondered? After all, they had the treasure map.

But Bones and Jones did not have
the map, because Portside, that
clever sea dog, had swapped it!
He had swapped it for Peg's
knitting pattern!

By the time he finally got home Patch was a very tired little pirate. He'd had quite enough adventure for one day.

Tomorrow, though, was
another story . . .
"Did I ever tell you about the
time I captured Casserole Jack
and his crew, single-handed,
armed only with a fish-slice
and a frying-pan . . . ?"

# ★ Pirate Patch ★

## ROSE IMPEY  NATHAN REED

Pirate Patch and the Black Bonnet Attack   978 1 84362 974 0

Pirate Patch and the Gallant Rescue   978 1 84362 975 7

Pirate Patch and the Chest of Bones   978 1 84362 976 4

Pirate Patch and the Message in a Bottle   978 1 84362 977 1

Pirate Patch and the Treasure Map   978 1 84362 978 8

Pirate Patch and the Great Sea Rescue   978 1 84362 979 5

Pirate Patch and the Five-minute Fortune   978 1 84362 980 1

Pirate Patch and the Abominable Pirates   978 1 84362 981 8

All priced at £8.99

Orchard Colour Crunchies are available from all good bookshops,
or can be ordered direct from the publisher:
Orchard Books, PO BOX 29, Douglas IM99 1BQ
Credit card orders please telephone 01624 836000
or fax 01624 837033 or visit our internet site: www.orchardbooks.co.uk
or e-mail: bookshop@enterprise.net for details.

To order please quote title, author and ISBN
and your full name and address.
Cheques and postal orders should be made payable to 'Bookpost plc.'
Postage and packing is FREE within the UK
(overseas customers should add £2.00 per book).

Prices and availability are subject to change.